MAY THE
BEST BOT WIN!

By Ryder Windham

Illustrated by Patrick Spaziante

Simon Spotlight

New York   London   Toronto   Sydney   New Delhi

SIMON SPOTLIGHT

An imprint of Simon & Schuster Children's Publishing Division

1230 Avenue of the Americas, New York, New York 10020

This Simon Spotlight edition December 2023

TRANSFORMERS and all related characters are trademarks of Hasbro and are used with permission. TRANSFORMERS © 2023 Hasbro. All Rights Reserved. Transformers: EarthSpark TV series © 2023 Hasbro/Viacom International Inc. All Rights Reserved. Nickelodeon is a trademark of Viacom International Inc.

All rights reserved, including the right of reproduction in whole or in part in any form. SIMON SPOTLIGHT and colophon are registered trademarks of Simon & Schuster, Inc. For information about special discounts for bulk purchases, please contact Simon & Schuster Special Sales at 1-866-506-1949 or business@simonandschuster.com.

Designed by Chrisila Maida

The illustrations for this book were rendered digitally.

The text of this book was set in Proxima Nova.

Manufactured in the United States of America 1123 LAK

10 9 8 7 6 5 4 3 2 1

ISBN 978-1-6659-4698-8 (hc)

ISBN 978-1-6659-4697-1 (pbk)

ISBN 978-1-6659-4699-5 (ebook)

CONTENTS

CHAPTER 1
SIBLINGS LIKE TO COMPETE

"Dad's home with Robby and Mo!" Twitch said. "Let's greet them!" She ran out of the Malto family's barn, quickly followed by Hashtag, Thrash, Nightshade, Jawbreaker, and Bumblebee. The first Transformers bots to be born on Earth, along with their trainer and friend, Bumblebee, came to a stop at the edge of the driveway, where they watched Alex, Robby, and

Mo Malto climb out of their van.

Bumblebee said, "How was school today?"

Robby held up a small metal trophy. "Check out this award!" he said. "My cloned-cabbage-leaf experiment won the science fair!"

"Won?" Mo said. "What a bragger! Your cloned leaf came in third place!"

"You're just jealous," Robby said, "because your fancy crystal-growing experiment didn't place at all."

"Ha!" Mo said. "How could my dazzling crystal geodes be jealous of your boring vegetables?"

"Because my cloned cabbages could help end world hunger," Robby said, "and my trophy is proof that my science project was better than yours!"

"Oh yeah?" Mo said. "I'm still stronger and faster than you! I challenge you to race me on the mile-long circle trail in the woods!"

"You're on!" Robby said. "Twitch and Thrash will be the referees, and Bumblebee will be the judge."

"I will?" Bumblebee said. "But—"

"Come on, Bumblebee," Mo said, "let's do this!"

Twitch rapidly changed to her

drone mode and hovered up into the air. "I'll watch the race from above," she said. "And I'll transmit video to Hashtag."

"Great idea!" Hashtag said. She extended her satellite dish and activated her tablet.

Twitch flew above the others as they went to the trail in the nearby woods. As Hashtag held her tablet

to display Twitch's aerial view, Nightshade turned to Alex and said, "Dad, why are Mo and Robby so frequently competitive?"

Alex chuckled. "Good question! When brothers and sisters compete, it's called *sibling rivalry*. It's their way of testing their skills and abilities with each other. It's totally normal."

Mo and Robby got ready to run. Thrash said, "Ready . . . set . . . go!"

Watching the two competitors sprint away, Jawbreaker said, "Who will win? The suspense is too much!" He covered his eyes.

Eleven minutes later Jawbreaker uncovered his eyes to see Mo run across the finish line on the circular trail. Two minutes after Bumblebee declared Mo the winner, Robby finished, almost out of breath. Robby said, "Congrats, Mo."

"Yes!" Mo said. "You admit I'm faster and stronger!"

"At least until our *next* race!" Robby said.

Nightshade muttered, "This sibling rivalry is strangely intriguing."

The group left the woods and returned home just as Dot Malto was climbing out of her park ranger truck. Alex said, "Honey, you're home early. Are you okay?"

"I'm fine," Dot said, "but Optimus Prime says he needs Bumblebee for

an emergency mission. Something about running into some Decepticon trouble."

"I'll leave at once," Bumblebee said, "but . . . who'll watch the Terrans?"

Just then a white race car zoomed into the driveway. The car stopped fast, changed into a tall Cybertronian robot, and said, "Optimus Prime sent me."

Wheeljack had arrived.

CHAPTER 2
LET THE GAMES BEGIN

The next day, while Robby and Mo were at school and Bumblebee was on his mission, the five Terrans walked up to Wheeljack as he repaired an old tractor in the barn. Seeing the Terrans, Wheeljack set aside his tools and said, "Something on your minds, kids?"

"Yesterday," Nightshade said, "we learned about sibling rivalry. And my

Terran siblings and I believe we might benefit from competing with each other. Because you are a scientist, we trust you to design a competition that tests our athleticism, intelligence, and creativity."

"A competition with three tests?" Wheeljack said. "That's called a *triathlon*. Do all five of you want to compete?"

Twitch said, "Thrash and I agreed that we shouldn't because we've been here on Earth a bit longer, so we've already had our share of sibling rivalry competitions."

"However," Thrash added, "Twitch

and I could help you judge the contestants!"

"Very well," Wheeljack said as he turned to the Terrans: Nightshade, known for their love of science; Hashtag, a proud fanatic of social media; and Jawbreaker, the gentle giant. "Your first challenge is to create a science presentation that explains how everything is made of matter but is also constantly changing form. You have one hour to complete this challenge."

The three Terrans descended to the Dugout, their underground headquarters beneath the barn, and

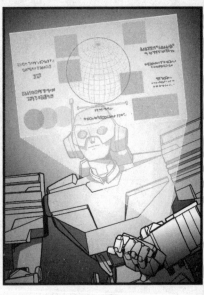

went straight to work. Jawbreaker created a diagram with paper and cardboard. Hashtag used her unlimited Internet access to create a digital presentation. Nightshade thought the challenge was too simple and decided instead to prepare a physical demonstration to prove that no form of matter in the universe could

travel faster than the speed of light.

An hour later Wheeljack, Twitch, and Thrash examined the three bots' presentations. When they were done, Wheeljack said, "The winner is . . . Hashtag."

Jawbreaker said, "Congratulations, Hashtag."

"Wow!" Hashtag said. "Thanks!"

Facing the judges, Nightshade said, "I don't wish to sound argumentative, but was my own presentation not more ambitious and technologically sophisticated?"

"It's Ambitious and sophisticated, yes," Wheeljack said, "but your presentation did not explain the nature of matter and how it changes form."

Twitch said, "Let's remember what Bumblebee taught us: it's important for our team to follow directions."

"Truth!" Thrash said. "If even one of us doesn't follow directions, the results could be dangerous for everyone!"

"Yes, I see," Nightshade said, and turned to Hashtag. "Congratulations, Hashtag, and please forgive me for not immediately acknowledging your accomplishment."

"It's okay. Don't worry about it!" Hashtag said.

Jawbreaker said, "What will the second challenge be, Mr. Wheeljack?"

"Meet me and the judges in the field

behind the barn in twenty minutes," Wheeljack said. Twitch and Thrash followed Wheeljack out of the barn.

Hashtag said, "Mo and Robby should be home soon. Maybe they can watch our competition!"

Nineteen minutes later Hashtag, Nightshade, and Jawbreaker heard two familiar voices from outside the barn. The first voice yelled, "Oh no!"

The second voice yelled, "Help! We're trapped!"

Jawbreaker gasped. "That sounds like Mo and Robby!"

Thinking their human siblings might be in danger, Nightshade, Hashtag, and Jawbreaker nearly tripped over each other as they raced out of the barn.

CHAPTER 3
SAVE US IF YOU CAN

When Nightshade, Hashtag, and Jawbreaker arrived at the field behind the barn, they were surprised to see a large wooden cage resting on an elevated platform, surrounded by rubber tires, cardboard boxes, scrap metal, and other odd items. They were even more surprised when they noticed the wooden cage was occupied by Mo and Robby, who

were smiling. Mo waved her hand between the bars of the cage and said, "Hi, guys!"

Hashtag said, "What's going on?"

"The second challenge!" Wheeljack said as he, Thrash, and Twitch stepped away from the side of the barn. Wheeljack faced Nightshade,

Hashtag, and Jawbreaker and said, "While you were working on your presentations earlier, I used scrap materials to build this obstacle course." Wheeljack gestured to the many odd items that surrounded the cage. "When Mo and Robby returned from school, I invited them to be

'captives' for this challenge. Terrans, you must use your strength, agility, and problem-solving skills to avoid the booby traps and liberate the captives."

Jawbreaker shifted back and forth on his large metal feet. "Because I'm a natural athlete," he said, "this should be a cinch."

Wheeljack said, "Everyone ready? Go!"

Wasting no time, Jawbreaker and Hashtag leaped into the obstacle course. Jawbreaker stepped onto a flattened sheet of metal, activating a concealed spring mechanism that launched him forward and into a web made from ropes. Hashtag tried to tiptoe across three rubber tires, but a wire hidden in the third tire snared her right foot, causing her to stumble into a stack of metal barrels.

While Jawbreaker and Hashtag struggled to free themselves from the ropes and barrels, Nightshade stood

quietly at the edge of the obstacle course and studied the various traps. Nightshade changed fast into their alt mode, a broad-winged hawk owl, and flew up and over the wooden cage at the middle of the obstacle course, avoiding the ropes meant to activate more booby traps. Grabbing the cage, Nightshade lifted it and carried Mo and Robby away from the traps. Nightshade landed and gently

placed the cage on the ground near Wheeljack, Thrash, and Twitch.

"We have a winner!" Wheeljack said as Twitch happily opened the cage and released Mo and Robby. "Congratulations, Nightshade!"

"Thank you," Nightshade said with a bow.

"Wait a minute," Hashtag said as she and Jawbreaker moved carefully out of the obstacle course.

"Nightshade barely had to touch the obstacle course, and Jawbreaker and I can't fly. Was this challenge fair?"

Wheeljack said, "Hashtag, I assure you that the challenge *was* fair. If you and Jawbreaker had taken a moment to survey the course instead of jumping right into it, you could have bypassed the traps and rescued the captives."

"Oh!" Hashtag said. "I should have

been more thoughtful and less hasty. Congrats to you, Nightshade, and well done."

"And now," Wheeljack said, "let us proceed to the third challenge!"

Jawbreaker sighed. He was feeling embarrassed because he hadn't won a single challenge, and he had only one more chance.

CHAPTER 4
A SURPRISING POEM

After leading the Terrans, Robby, and Mo into the Dugout, Wheeljack said, "For the final challenge of this triathlon, we shall test your creativity."

"Creativity?" Hashtag said. "I'm loaded with creativity! For the next challenge, I wish we could make a dance video, and then—"

"Thank you for that interesting suggestion, Hashtag," Wheeljack interrupted, "but I've already decided the details of this particular challenge. Each of you has ten minutes to write a haiku, which is a type of poetry that originated in Japan. A haiku consists of three lines, with words that add up to five syllables in the first line, seven syllables in the second, and five syllables in the third. The words

do not have to rhyme, and you may repeat words if you like. Punctuation and capitalization are not required."

Jawbreaker said, "If it's not too much to ask, Mr. Wheeljack, maybe you could give us an example?"

"Of course," Wheeljack said. "I've composed a rather simple haiku for that very purpose." He pointed to a

sheet of paper on a bulletin board. On the paper Wheeljack had written:

heavy winds may cause

a bird to fly the wrong way

sometimes for the best

"I admit," Wheeljack said, "it's a very simple haiku. I expect *better* from you. Your goal is to compose a haiku

that will resonate with everyone in this room." He handed out paper and pencils to Hashtag, Nightshade, and Jawbreaker. "You may begin . . . now!"

Nightshade completed their haiku in just seventeen seconds. Hashtag completed her own haiku eleven seconds later. Jawbreaker wrote very, very slowly, sometimes pausing between words to use his fingers to count the syllables. He did not put down his pencil until one second before Wheeljack said, "Time's up! Nightshade, please recite your haiku."

Nightshade said, "I believe you'll all appreciate my technical approach to this challenge." They continued:

"Five syllables plus
seven syllables plus five
more make a haiku."

Nightshade bowed. Wheeljack said, "Thank you, Nightshade. Now let us hear from Hashtag."

"Before I begin," Hashtag said with a bright smile, "I'd like to dedicate my haiku to all my friends!" She proceeded:

"Down in the Dugout,
when the music starts playing,
everyone gets DOWN!"

Hashtag busted a move. Wheeljack said, "Thank you, Hashtag. Finally, Jawbreaker, it's your turn."

Jawbreaker frowned. "I'm afraid it's probably not very good." Without much confidence, he read:

"Transforming ourselves can be hard, but we all must change for the better."

When Jawbreaker looked up from

his writing, he saw everyone gazing at him in silence. Then Twitch and Thrash glanced at Wheeljack and nodded.

Nightshade said, "Incredible."

Hashtag said, "Wow. Just wow."

Wheeljack said, "Jawbreaker, your haiku was . . . very moving."

Jawbreaker slumped. "Moving in a bad way?"

"On the contrary," Wheeljack said, "you *won*, Jawbreaker."

Jawbreaker said, "I did? Really?"

Then, everyone cheered. Jawbreaker turned to Nightshade and Hashtag and said, "Hugs all around!"

CHAPTER 5
FAMILY CELEBRATION

Dot and Alex Malto arrived home at the same time that Bumblebee returned from his mission with Optimus Prime. Standing in the driveway, they heard loud and happy voices coming from inside the barn. Bumblebee said, "Sounds like the kids are having a party!"

"But they forgot to invite us!" Alex said.

Dot, Alex, and Bumblebee went into the barn. They found Wheeljack watching Mo, Robby, and the five Terrans as they ran around, laughing and shouting. Hashtag came to a stop and said, "Mom! Dad! Bumblebee! We had a sibling rivalry triathlon!"

Twitch said, "Thrash and I were judges along with Wheeljack!"

Thrash said, "Hashtag, Nightshade, and Jawbreaker competed, and each won a test!"

Hashtag said, "I won the science presentation!"

Nightshade said, "Next, I won the obstacle course!"

Jawbreaker said, "And I won for being creative!"

"Really?" Alex said. "Kids, that's terrific! And also . . . unexpected! For a science presentation, I would have guessed Nightshade to win. For an obstacle course, I would have guessed Jawbreaker. And for creativity, I would have guessed Hashtag."

Hashtag said, "Dad, before the triathlon, I think all of us would have

guessed the same way as you!"

Nightshade said, "I daresay this new experience was simultaneously thrilling and enlightening."

Jawbreaker nodded and said, "We kind of surprised ourselves, as well as each other." The Terrans hugged their human parents.

Wheeljack said, "Again, I extend my

hearty congratulations to Hashtag, Jawbreaker, and Nightshade. But I feel compelled to point out that when a competition ends in a tie, it is customary to have an additional test, a tiebreaker, to determine a single winner."

Mo said, "I have a better idea! Let's start a whole new triathlon, only this

time Robby, Twitch, Thrash, and I can compete too!"

Thrash said, "I like that idea! We could start with a high-speed race!"

Twitch said, "And Mom and Dad can be the judges, and we—"

Dot let out a loud whistle and everyone immediately settled down and stopped talking.

"Excuse me," she said, "but I'd like to know . . . where did you kids get the idea of competing with each other?"

"From Dad," Nightshade said. "Yesterday he said that sibling rivalry was a totally normal way of testing skills and abilities."

Dot raised her eyebrows. Looking at Alex, she said, "Is that right?"

"Well," Alex said, "yes, I believe I did say something like that."

"I see," Dot said. "Kids, I know competitions can be fun, and also educational, but let's keep in mind that siblings take care of each other, and that everyone in our family is on the same team. Agreed?"

The seven Malto children nodded and then everyone squeezed in for a group hug. But then Hashtag said, "Mom, I have an idea for a fun contest, and everyone who participates will win."

"Oh?" Dot said. "And what contest is that?"

Hashtag pulled out her video

camera, blasted music from her speakers, and said, "Malto family dance contest!"

Wheeljack smiled as Hashtag's wish for a dance video "challenge" finally came true.

Ready for another  adventure?

Here's a sneak peek of Book 4,

NO MALTO LEFT BEHIND!

Standing next to the Transformers robot Bumblebee, Dot Malto faced her seven children and said, "Listen up, Maltos. Optimus Prime has given us a mission!"

The Malto children included Mo, her brother Robby, and their Terran siblings: Twitch, Thrash, Hashtag, Nightshade, and Jawbreaker. They had been playing tag outside the large barn on their family's farm, but now they gave their full attention to their mother and Bumblebee. Their father, Alex Malto, stepped out of the house and asked, "What's going on?"